I0640941

Firebrand Firestorm

The Ancestors of Bjorn Esterday

Volume 14

Wisdom

JULY 4, 1776

Wynter Sommers

Wynter Sommers

This work is registered with the UK Copyright Service, in
accordance with the Copyright, Designs and Patents Act 1988
All rights reserved 284718040

USA Copyright © 2015 GJ dePillis
© 2015, TXu001966602 / 2015-05-08 and TXu001983965 / 2015-11-04

Library of Congress Control Number: 2020943167

Published by Pure Force Enterprises, Inc.
California, USA
Since 2002

INGRAM

INGRAM® Distribution

ISBN-13: 978-1-7184-0026-9
ISBN-10: 1-7184-0026-8

DEDICATION

To those who feel strongly about truth, justice, and the integrity of America; your honorable actions make us proud. To those who wonder if their daily choices matter; your small decisions impact generations to come. To those everyday people who don't think they have what it takes; when you strive for extraordinary things, the impossible becomes reality. Your dreams today become our future tomorrow. Thank you for everything you do.

Bjorn Esterday
Was Not Born Yesterday
Series

Firebrand (15 Volumes+Conversation Station Book)
Edges (9 Stories +Conversation Station Book)
Gone (18 Stories + Conversation Station Book)

Bjorn EDGES Series
EDGES Book 1-Swift Encounter
EDGES Book 2-Rousing Attack
EDGES Book 3-One Foot Under
EDGES Book 4-Earthshake
EDGES Book 5-Broken String
EDGES Book 6-Key Witness
EDGES Book 7-Who is She?
EDGES Book 8-Vanish
EDGES Book 9-Chase or Die

Bjorn Series Alternate Reading Plan

1st	Edges Book 1		22nd	Gone Book 10
2nd	Edges Book 2		23rd	Firebrand Vol 9
3rd	Gone Book 1		24rd	Gone Book 11
4th	Firebrand Vol 1		25th	Firebrand Vol 10
5th	Edges Book 3		26th	Gone Book 12
6th	Firebrand Vol 2		27th	Gone Book 13
7th	Gone Book 2		28th	Firebrand Vol 11
8th	Gone Book 3		29th	Gone Book 14
9th	Firebrand Vol 3		30th	Firebrand Vol 12
10th	Gone Book 4		31st	Gone Book 15
11th	Firebrand Vol 4		32nd	Firebrand Vol 13
12th	Gone Book 5		33rd	Gone Book 16
13th	Gone Book 6		34th	Firebrand Vol 14
14th	Edges Book 4		35th	Gone Book 17
15th	Firebrand Vol 5		36th	Firebrand Vol15 (End)
16th	Gone Book 7		37th	Gone Book 18 (End)
17th	Firebrand Vol 6		38th	Edges Book 5
18th	Gone Book 8		39th	Edges Book 6
19th	Firebrand Vol 7		40th	Edges Book 7
20th	Gone Book 9		41st	Edges Book 8
21st	Firebrand Vol 8		42nd	Edges Book 9(End)

ACKNOWLEDGMENTS

We acknowledge those who actively build peace. We acknowledge all the selfless talent which contributed to creating meaningful tokens of consideration and sharing. We acknowledge that every person has a daily choice of right or wrong... and we thank you for choosing the right, good, honorable path filled with integrity because that is the difficult and brave path. Small choices today become lasting monuments of loving hope tomorrow.

CONTENTS

CHARACTERS..1

♦※ LOCATIONS※♦...5

0 PREFACE...7

1 CHAPTER 141: (JULY 4, 1776) Come Inside the Church,
Says the Magistrate...8

2 CHAPTER 142: (JULY 3, 1776) Hours Earlier aboard the
SPY...20

3 CHAPTER 143: (JULY 3, 1776): Jane Dangles...................27

4 CHAPTER 144: (JULY 3, 1776) Just After That...............31

5 CHAPTER 145: (JULY 4, 1776) The Search Continues for
Bryce, Early Morning..37

6 CHAPTER 146: (JULY 4, 1776) Pew Pondering. How did
You Survive?..44

7 CHAPTER 147: (JULY 4, 1776) Jane Wanted to See the
Document Signed..52

8 CHAPTER 148: (JULY 4, 1776) The Second Proposal........67

9 CHAPTER 149: (JULY 4, 1776) The Meeting Adjourns.....72

10 CHAPTER 150: (JULY 4, 1776) Getting the Carriage.....80

11 What Just Happened?..97

12 Did You Know...99

13 Vocabulary..117

CHARACTERS

♥ **Billy Dawes**- the carriage driver who befriends Silversmith.

♥ **Bryce Aiden** Tyler- Jane's Uncle Floyd's business partner

♥ **Button Gwinette** – the husband of Polly. Button defended his cabin during an attack to allow Polly, his wife, to escape. Button came to the Colonies to work in Georgia, where he owns land. When he married Polly, their land straddled the corners of Maryland Colony and Delaware Colony.

♥ **Eliza Lucas**- a young rugged girl who is experimenting with developing Indigo dye to counteract the red coats of the British. Her father has a rice plantation in the South Carolina colony and she believes Lady Sarah Wilson is not to be trusted.

♥ **Eunice Williams**, later known as *Marguerite Kanenstenhawi Arosen, of the Bear tribe.* Eunice married a man from the Wolf tribe. She was taken as a girl and raised as a native American also called "Indian'.

1

♥ **Henry Mossop**- a former opera star who has fallen on hard times and now wants to make profits in another way. He left Ireland, due to failed business and growing debt, and is now friends with Lady Sarah Wilson

♥ **Jane Hargreaves**- Once socially well positioned in England, her parents died, leaving all their wealth to the nearest married male relative, resulting in Jane becoming penniless save for a small allowance. She had to discharge an entire household of staff, save Silversmith. Uncle Floyd sponsored Jane and Silversmith to voyage to the Colonies to live with him in Dover, Delaware.

♥ **Magistrate Karl Pinkney** - the official who works with Bryce to find out the truth. Karl has a brother who had to liquidate all his assets and send the proceeds to the King's Treasury. Karl is trying to find out why his brother was accused of a crime, yet cannot find out the nature of this crime.

♥ **Mr. Tweedbottom**- The tailor in town who is enamored with Jane Hargreaves

♥ **Mrs. Elizabeth Dunlap** – the wife of John Dunlap, Mrs. Dunlap allowed Polly to stay in their home in exchange for Bacoun (bacon).

♥ **Mr. John Dunlap**- He was born in Strabane, Pennsylvania. After he apprenticed as a printer, he set up shop in Philadelphia where he lives with his wife, Elizabeth.

♥ **Peter Timothy**- Son of Elizabeth Timothy, who wrote the book *Reflections on Courtship and Marriage* later attributed to Ben Franklin. He helps Silversmith and Billy Dawes to get closer to their goal.

♥ **Polly Mulhoolin**– the wife of Button Gwinette . They live in the undeveloped area West of New Castle, Delaware and North of Kent County and East of Cecil County in Maryland.

♥ **Sarah Wilson**- a woman of questionable past who has befriended Henry Mossop.

♥ **Silversmith**- Lady's maid and companion who travelled with Jane Hargreaves from England.

♥ **Simms**- Mr. and Mrs. Dunlap's butler

♥ **Susanna Wright**- an educated woman who organizes secret meetings, the last of which occurred in a barn. She makes silk, and helps her community in many capacities. She is from the Susquehanna River area in Pennsylvania.

♥ **TallMan** –the son of Eunice Williams; travelling medicine man

♥ **Uncle Floyd Hargreaves** – Jane's Uncle, who paid full passage for both Jane and her maid Silversmith, from England to his home in Dover, Delaware in the colonies in the New World

♥ **Witherspoon**- butler to Jane's Uncle Floyd.

LOCATIONS

♣ Philadelphia: Home to John & Elizabeth **Dunlap.**

♣ Philadelphia: The **State House** where the Declaration of Independence was signed.

♣ Philadelphia: Location of **The Inn.**

♣ Somewhere near or around Philadelphia: **Meeting Town**

♣ Canada: Where Tallman and his mother Eunice are from.

♣ Rising Sun, Maryland: Lady Sarah **Wilson's Estate**.

♣ Dover, Delaware: **Hargreaves Home.** Uncle Floyd lived there and invited Jane, with her lady's maid Silversmith, to live there also.

♣ South Carolina Colony: **Eliza Lucas** is from this area.

♣ Susquehanna, Pennsylvania: **Susanna Wright** is from this area.

♣ Maryland/Delaware Colonies: **Polly Mulhoolin, wife to Button Gwinette.** Both live in the open wooded area straddling the Maryland and Delaware colonies.

0 PREFACE

So much has happened. Jane is about to share the story as to why Silversmith, was so valuable in unknowingly helping Jane return so that she might tell the story.   We see how an act of consideration long ago actually could save the dignity and life of another.

1 CHAPTER 141: (JULY 4, 1776) Come Inside the Church, Says the Magistrate

"What happened?" Billy Dawes asked, stunned as Polly and Silversmith stared, speechless.

There standing on the deserted streets, in the city of Philadelphia, in the colony of Pennsylvania, near the State House, in which the Continental Congress was meeting, stood Magistrate Karl Pinkney, Eliza Lucas, Silversmith, Polly with her newborn babe, and Billy Dawes.

Now, Magistrate Pinkney had just assisted two new people out of the carriage. The small group halted on the deserted streets in front of the church.

Amused, Magistrate Pinkney smiled and looked at Eliza.

"Mr. Tyler!" Polly exclaimed. "We have not seen you since you had tea at Mrs. Dunlap's parlor. You were searching for Jane..."

"Who," Jane announced, "Is happy to see you, Polly." Jane, barely recognizable, took a step toward her friend, but stumbled.

Magistrate Karl Pinkney explained, "Although she valiantly tries, Miss Hargreaves is not able to walk on her own," he cautioned. Bryce reached out to aid Jane. She leaned against him for support. Her body was sore and battered.

Magistrate Pinkney waved the carriage toward the others, which were parked around the State House, where the

Continental Congress was meeting. With efficiency, Karl Pinkney, Magistrate, gently ushered the party into the empty church, first pulling open massive doors and looking inside.

"Appears to be empty," Magistrate Pinkney shared. "We can sit inside in the pews."

Jane's torn dress still dragged a trail of water behind it along the stone floor. Bryce helped her carefully to a seated position in one of the pews. Slowly, the group funneled inside the church and sat upon the cold wooden benches.

Jane smiled, "I want to thank God in His House for sparing my life, and rejoining me with my friends... and for discovering the answers I sought about Uncle Floyd. It was not an easy journey."

"May we ask what happened, Miss Jane?" Billy Dawes, curious, gently prodded, trying to hide his gruff side.

"Of course, Mr. Dawes," Jane started, "It is a tale I can scarcely believe myself." She looked at Silversmith, "Your first mission, Silversmith. You executed it brilliantly."

"Mr. Dawes," Silversmith assured Jane, "Has been respectful and guarded me during the entire quest, Miss Jane."

Jane turned to Billy Dawes, "Then, I dare say, I may need to consider you a permanent member of our household, should you wish it, Mr. Dawes."

Billy said nothing but grinned, then blushed, then nodded. Then, he shot a coy glance at Silversmith and their gaze lingered.

Bryce Aiden Tyler, now spoke, "Jane just told me she owes her life to you, Silversmith."

"I thank you, Mr. Bryce, but I confess I do not understand." Silversmith uttered, "I've been at the inn and with... I don't understand... Last I saw Miss Jane was when she told me to find you and Magistrate Pinkney. Then, when I showed you where they were, Magistrate Pinkney sent me to the inn with one of his men."

Jane explained, "To summarize it all, Mr. Mossop, the opera singer, had allied himself with Lady Sarah Wilson, who was never actually appointed the title of 'Lady', and the two of them started a business based on ignoring human dignity."

"I don't understand," Polly shared.

Bryce added, "Magistrate Pinkney and I questioned Henry Mossop and found he was funded from the King's treasury."

Polly gasped, "Indeed?"

Bryce continued, "They would send word to England about which settlers seemed prosperous, but not powerful. Then those people would be arrested for no reason, and later presented with two options."

Polly asked, "Which two options were offered these falsely accused victims?"

Bryce enumerated, "One: go to prison or, two: liquidate all their earned assets and send the proceeds to the King's Treasury across the ocean to England."

Polly exclaimed, "To be punished for a crime never committed? The Bible is clear about how wrong are such false accusations and cruel theft!"

Silversmith added, "The seventeenth chapter of the good book of wisdom, says, *'He that justifieth the wicked, and he that condemneth the just, even they both are an abomination to the Lord'...* verse fifteen, that was. Proverbs."

"Quite right, Silversmith," Jane replied, "But with that funding, Mr. Mossop hired men, such as that pretentious Mr. Tweedbottom. He was already in debt due to feeling entitled to the wealth and luxuries of others he envied and yearned to posses at any cost...even the lives of innocents."

Silversmith added, "I overheard two men talking to Henry Mossop in the fields of the barn at that last meeting which was raided by the King's men. If Mr. Tweedbottom was one of them, who was the other man?"

Magistrate Pinkney assured, "As Bryce and I were questioning Henry Mossop, my soldiers found the other fellow waiting for Mr. Mossop at the docks. The other fellow is now in a prison cell, just like Henry Mossop. When I return, I will see to it they shall stand trial."

"And what of Mr. Tweedbottom?" Silversmith asked, "Won't he be held accountable for what he's done?"

"He already has paid," Eliza Lucas replied. "With his life. I saw him go overboard and later, his body was recovered during the search efforts which Magistrate Pinkney had executed to rescue Jane and Mr. Tyler."

Magistrate Pinkney added, "In that unusual short storm, only one died. We recovered everybody else. Luckily, the Spy ship was close to shore and sank very slowly. It did not create a whirlpool which would have pulled down those who were trying to rescue the victims."

"Then, how," Silversmith asked Bryce Aiden Tyler, "Did I save Miss Jane?"

Eliza Lucas popped in, "I witnessed Mr. Tweedbottom throw our brave Miss Jane Hargreaves overboard."

"Over what board?" Silversmith asked.

Eliza clarified, "He *jettisoned* her. Pushed Jane...Miss Hargreaves... over the side of the ship!"

Silversmith puzzled, persisted, "Pardon me for thinking this, but if Miss Hargreaves were thrown into the waters, would not her dress become heavy laden with the water? My Miss Jane would sink as if she were a rock, would she not?"

Bryce explained, "Yes, Miss Hargreaves' skirts would have become so heavy with the water that she would have been pulled under to her death." Bryce paused, "But, Silversmith, you may not realize what an inventor you are..."

"Pardon?" Billy Dawes prodded.

Sunlight flickered through the stained glass windows of the church and cast a rainbow of lights onto Jane, drenching her in a cacophony of warm golden hues dotted with rays of azure blue and red accents.

Jane turned her face upward to welcome the warmth streaming in on dusty beams of light, then falling on those friendly faces clustered together in the pews.

Jane rested a hand on Silversmith's shoulder and said, "Silversmith, your ingenuity..."

She paused and then looked into the faces of the others .

Jane took a deep breath, then spoke, "Before I left London, I was wealthy. My parents died and my inheritance went to a distant cousin, leaving me penniless. Silversmith was the only one who stayed by my side and endured the rough journey to these colonies. She had tended to my vanities and frivolous addiction to fashion."

"Oh, Miss Jane... I could not have done this mission and found Susanna Wright had it not been for you teaching me to read and write so I could send you notes of our progress."

"And," Jane replied, "It was your note which summoned me here, which led me to meet Eliza Lucas and Susanna Wright... But you, Silversmith, you created a unique pannier substitute because mine broke in the journey over here, do you remember?"

"Oh!" Silversmith recalled, "Indeed! I spent forever and a day on sewing a new pannier. Mr. Witherspoon helped me. He is the best butler I've worked with." Then she lowered her voice, "But, Miss Jane... should we be talking about the undergarments of a lady in the company of men?"

"Yes, Silversmith..." Jane affirmed, "These people need to know how foolish I was to have allowed Mr. Tweedbottom's flippant comment about my lopsided silhouette make me ask you to drop everything just to build a new pannier. I wanted to be accepted so much that I was blind and beguiled by his flattering words. Mr. Tweedbottom only wanted to distract me, you, Silversmith and Uncle Floyd's butler, Witherspoon."

"Why?" Silversmith asked.

Jane replied solemnly, "So, Mr. Tweedbottom could murder Uncle Floyd... I gave him my Uncle's life in exchange for a derisive comment about my broken French Cage."

Eliza embraced Jane, "Oh, you are not to blame for the wicked and deceitful way in which Mr. Tweedbottom comported himself. He has paid for it with his life. No trial needed."

"French cage?" Billy asked.

Silversmith leaned toward Billy and whispered, "The pannier is what a lady wears underneath her skirts to give her hips the proper breadth in accordance to her social standing in respected society..."

Jane patted Eliza's hand, and continued, "Perhaps, I had best explain from the point Eliza last saw me speaking to Mr. Tweedbottom aboard the Spy ship."

2 CHAPTER 142: (JULY 3, 1776)
Hours Earlier aboard the SPY

"Mere hours ago," Jane started, "Eliza and I were aboard the Spy ship during the storm."

Eliza looked at the others sitting in the empty church, and explained, "I overheard the conversation Mr. Tweedbottom and Jane were having. I had to make a choice. Do I help Jane? Do I help those poor slaves trapped below deck? It seemed as if Jane had calmed Mr. Tweedbottom, engaging him in conversation, so I aided the prisoners. Only later did Mr. Tweedbottom admit he had thrown Jane over the side of the boat... all to protect his new profitable slave trade."

"Jane! Jane!" Eliza called refusing to believe that Mr. Tweedbottom had actually picked up the woman he claimed to love, and just threw her overboard! The wind whipped Eliza's words away, so they fell only on the ears of Mr. Tweedbottom. The rain fell with stinging accuracy.

With rage lacing her voice, Eliza Lucas charged at Mr. Tweedbottom slipping on deck as she honed in on her target shouting, "Where is Jane? What did you do with Jane?"

"She joined her Uncle," was all Tweedbottom said.

"You sacrificed Jane for this?" Eliza swept her arms around her to show this Mr. Tweedbottom the foolish destruction his impatient selfish desires for speedy riches and entitlement had caused.

The Spy ship and all that was on it, was slowly sinking.

Jane had fallen overboard, but the coils of rope in which she stood to brace herself against the rocking ship, unwound as gravity pulled her toward the yawning ocean. She must have stepped inside a small noose which tightened around her ankle as she plummeted toward the raging sea.

The rope had miraculously twisted and kinked in such a manner that it stopped short of allowing Jane to hit the water. With her ankle in the tangled rope, her skirts had fallen upside down, making her look like a bell to be rung. The rope held her face barely above the surface so Jane could feel the spray of salt water hit her face and hair, but she was still able to breathe.

Her ankle started to feel numb, circulation being restricted in a noose of rope.

The ledge of the railing jutted out and when Jane looked up, her upside down skirts prevented her from seeing.

Soon, Jane saw another end of a lax stretch of rope flopping about just out of her reach.

With all the strength Jane could muster, she tried to grab the rain soaked rope, but when it neared her hand, it gave her such a bite, she felt as if she had just been lashed with a whip. Ignoring the pain, she would push herself off the side of the ship and grab for the flopping rope again.

The next time she grasped it, she felt it in the palm of her hand, but it slipped out.

When the Spy ship encountered another wave, which rocked it up to a steep angle, more ropes from the coils on deck fell down as if a kitten were playing with a ball of spun yarn. She heard the ropes slapping against the side of the ship all around her.

The third time, she aimed for the rope, stretched for it, finally grabbing hold with both hands, but then the storm slammed her body against the side of the ship, stunning the breath out of her, and she released her grasp.

Not deterred in the slightest, Jane Hargreaves looked up and noticed the rope holding her ankle was tight, kinked and rigid. Her face was still well above water. She had time to try and grab that rope a fourth time.

Close to the water, Jane's fabric skirts ripped as part of them were pulled and dragged under the boat. She felt herself being hauled down, but the rope supporting her ankle remained ridged.

The rope slapped against Jane, this time, she took a deep breath and grabbed it. Just as she clung to the rope with both hands, the noose supporting her ankle suddenly un-kinked and became lax, flipping Jane right side up.

Next, Jane looked up and saw the rope with the noose around her ankle, how now fully fallen from the deck above her.

With a tiny splash, this rope tumbled into the waves below.

While dangling, Jane used her free leg to push off the noose on her ankle with her other foot, lest it pull her down. With little success, she pulled up her leg and quickly released one hand to reach down to her foot.

The cold water numbed her fingers and she could barely move them. Jane used her hand like a stiff hook. She lost dexterity of her knuckles and mobility of her lady-like fingers.

Finally, the noose around her ankle slipped off and silently plopped into the water.

She grasped the rope with both hands, wondering what to do next. Then, the ship tilted and slammed her against the side of the boat, but this time she clung to that rope and did not let go.

"Eliza," Jane called out, but who could hear over all the wind and rain. She thought she had heard Eliza call her name, but she couldn't be sure.

"Eliza, Eliza," Jane cried out again, but the words were snatched from her throat and flung to the churning watery abyss where nobody could hear Jane's pleas for succor.

3 CHAPTER 143: (JULY 3, 1776): Jane Dangles

Now upright, Jane dangled from a rope she desperately grasped on her fourth attempt. This rope supported her weight, for the time being... until it too would fall as the other rope had done.

She hung like drying laundry, clinging to this rope as it swayed along the hull of the ship. But her body was sliding slowly into the swirling sea.

Her water logged outer skirt fabric was gradually drawing Jane beneath the surface. Jane resisted. She kept her head above water. Then, Jane heard a loud RIIIIP as a portion of her skirt tore away.

Even if Jane had both hands free, which she did not as she clung to the rope to stay above water, on this stormy night, Jane would not be able to fumble with the strings or busk of her corset.

This is why, she thought at this moment, a lady's maid was required for dressing and undressing. The bum roll, which Silversmith had crafted for her, now half sprung loose and dangled, one end attached to Jane's waist and the other end flopping about in the wind. Jane was not wearing sea faring clothing.

The fires above illuminated the debris in the waters below.

She suddenly noticed a very thick rope floating nearby. There appeared to be bags attached to it, causing the rope to remain on the surface. Jane wondered why these bags did not sink, but rather floated.

Suddenly, appearing away over there, Jane caught a point of light.

Was it a boat? A lantern glowing in these cloudy inky skies? Could it be a place toward which she could swim?

Ah, yes, she did not know how to swim. Not ladylike, apparently, so she had been taught.

Faintly, Jane heard her name being called by her friend, Eliza Lucas.

"Jane, Jane..."

Jane tried to reply, but her words were choked by slaps of water hitting Jane in the face and all Jane could muster was a choking sound.

Jane looked up and could see the name of the ship painted above her, S-P-Y.

Behind the planks on which it was painted, danced flickers of light. The fire was consuming the entire vessel.

CRACK.

Jane looked above her and the very plank of wood holding the rope she was hanging onto for dear safety, the one right below the painted sign of the ship, now broke off.

Jane felt herself lowered into the icy cold waters with a splash.

Her rope had broken free.

Jane succumbed to her fate.

4 CHAPTER 144: (JULY 3, 1776) Just After That...

Bryce, who had just freed the wine merchant's ship's rudder from the tangled rope dotted with cork- filled sacks, now swam toward the Spy ship.

He was cautious to avoid getting too close, lest the sinking ship pull him down, as well. He did get too close, however and just heard the crack of wood splintering above him.

He noticed the sign of the ship S-P-Y as it cracked off and splashed over his head, giving him mere seconds to hold his breath and retreat beneath the surface to safety.

After he came to his senses and scrambled aboard the wooden debris, he saw it had the name of the vessel on it, Spy.

This would be his raft.

From here, he could paddle over to several victims and save them, which he did. Then, Bryce Aiden Tyler noticed his raft was blocked by a mass of brocade fabric.

As Bryce plunged his hand into the water again, he felt the silky long strands of what he now realized was hair from a woman's head.

As quickly as he could, Bryce pulled the fabric with all his might. With fire-light dancing from the smoldering inferno nearby, Bryce saw that he was pulling in an unconscious woman, who had miraculously remained afloat in her under skirts.

He pulled the body of this woman onto his tiny raft.

Was she dead? Drowned? Or did she have some breath still in her?

Bryce, seeing his cork-bag rope drifting away, lunged to grab it before it got too far, but all he could grab was one of the bags, which ripped free from the main tether.

As Bryce Aiden Tyler saw the rope float away, he noticed he needed to push clear of this ship quickly before it went down.

He and his new passenger were in danger of either being hit by more falling debris, or of being sucked down beneath the surface with the ship.

Neither was an appealing option.

Now, with no tether to lead him back to the dot of light, that lantern aboard the wine merchant's boat, Bryce slipped half his body into the water and while grasping onto the wooden raft, he kicked with all his might propelling himself in any direction away from the sinking ship.

Then, a large wave reared up like a boggled horse, which had been startled by an aggressive fox.

The wave crashed down on top of Bryce and his makeshift raft, which splintered beneath them.

Refusing to release the unconscious woman, Bryce Aiden Tyler found the laces of her corset on her back and wrapped the loops around his arm.

Without letting go, Bryce kept his head above water along with his unconscious female companion.

He noticed the dot of light from the wine merchant's ship was farther away, now. Disoriented, Bryce tried to get a sense of where he was.

The wave had pushed them some distance from the blazing inferno, keeping them both safe from falling debris as well as the suction caused by a sinking ship.

Unfortunately, it had also transported them further from the wine merchant's ship. The dot of hopeful light emanating from the lantern aboard the wine merchant's boat was getting smaller and smaller.

Now, the rain had stopped and the clouds were beginning to fade. Was dawn approaching? In the watery light cast by the moon and rising sun, he noticed this woman was breathing. That was a good sign.

The pressure of her weight against the laces, which he had wrapped around his forearm, were beginning to cut off his circulation.

He quickly noticed a loose bum roll floating from her waist. Bryce grabbed this bum roll as he slipped his hand out of the lace loops. Still keeping the bum roll attached to her waist, Bryce laid the bum roll along his forearm and then slipped the loops of the woman's corsets around his forearm.

He kept his other hand on the cork-filled bag he had ripped from the lead rope earlier.

Padding from the bum roll distributed the pressure of the woman's weight from the corset laces, which had been biting into his flesh.

The numbness was now lessened.

Bryce refused to release his grip on the unconscious woman.

He started to push her hair from her face to see who she was, and allow her to breathe more easily.

5 CHAPTER 145: (JULY 4, 1776) The Search Continues for Bryce, Early Morning

Doubt was pierced with urgency as the Magistrate's men scrambled aboard the wine merchant's vessel in the now calming, but still turbulent waters.

Some of the row boats had dropped off survivors to this boat instead of going all the way back to shore and returning. Others headed to shore.

The wine merchant's boat was filling up with exhausted, wet, cold, yet grateful colonists.

They had all been kidnapped and scheduled to be sold as slaves. The catastrophe they had just barely survived meant a second chance for them to return to their families.

Amidst the chaos of boarding the victims of Henry Mossop's slave trade, the men shouted to each other, "What are we to do?"

Another responded, "We need to wait for Mr. Tyler. If it weren't for him untangling the rudder, this vessel would have sunk."

Another called out, "And we would not have been able to save these people."

Yet one more cried out with determination, "We will not give up on Mr. Tyler. We must wait."

"But we are filling up!" Another cried, "We cannot take on more survivors. We risk our own lives if we remain."

"Then send the rowboats straight to shore." The other admonished, "We won't risk any more, but we do need to remain and wait."

"Why not," Another suggested, "pull in the lead rope as he may be clinging to it."

The others looked at each other.

As they worked to pull up the last survivor, they also ordered each rowboat approaching to head directly to shore.

They next worked to pull in the slack from the rope, which still had tied to it those cork-filled bags now floating on the surface of the angry waters.

While some appointed themselves to ensuring the boat did not take on water from aggressively lapping waves, others were securing the rescued victims, two guarded the helm, and the remainder put their backs into hauling the heavy water logged rope aboard.

These volunteers from Magistrate Karl Pinkney were exhausted. Even with the palms of their hands bloody and raw, their sheer dedication fueled them to move forward with the tasks at hand.

One leaned over with a lantern to see if anybody could be seen in the water. He returned with a shake of his head and downcast eyes.

There was a silence among the red-coated men who had volunteered for this venture. Finally, one broke the silence with, "I saw him climb aboard a portion of the Spy ship. I saw it fall and I saw him climb onto it and float."

"Aye," Another agreed, "He used it to push the cork bags over to these victims so they could stay afloat until the rowboats got to them. I refuse to believe that Mr. Tyler wouldn't grab one of his own cork bags."

Another pointed into the water, "Is that the debris on which Bryce Aiden Tyler had climbed?"

The men rushed to the side of the wine merchant's boat and leaned as far over as they could.

It was half of the wooden name plate, which had fallen from the ship. The wooden fragment drifted toward the wine merchant's boat as if to oblige the men so they could read it.

Then, it hit the side of the hull with a "THUNK".

The man holding the lantern, leaned over to make sure it was the Spy Ship name and... it was. Slowly, he turned to meet his comrades with a grim expression.

One solemnly said, "He fought the ocean with bravery. We can let Magistrate Pinkney know."

Another concurred with a grimace, "We cannot brave this storm any longer without peril to us all."

The others who had continued to pull in the rope called out, "It's empty. No soul clings to the rope."

The most senior of the men aboard the wine merchant's boat stepped forward and clearly shouted above the winds, "Spread out and search the waters all around. If Mr. Tyler is not tied to that rope, he may be holding onto one of the floating cork filled bags. But if you do not see him in the next few moments, we do need to return to shore."

Suddenly, splashing waves came up from behind them, a direction they were not expecting, tossing the boat, causing the occupants to scream and scramble to hold on to something so they would not slide off.

"We must head back to shore now or we will all die out here! Bryce will be remembered as the one who saved all these men and women!" The man hoped he sounded reassuring.

Wind whipped around their heavy hearts and pushed them toward a decision. It was time to leave and save all who were aboard the wine merchant's boat.

The senior red coat shouted one last order, "As anchor is pulled up, you have that time to scour the seas with your eyes in search of a man who just might still be alive... and then we return to shore!"

The men reluctantly started to pull up the anchor... slowly

6 CHAPTER 146: (JULY 4, 1776) Pew Pondering. How did You Survive?

Silversmith found herself entranced by the warm rainbow of colors streaming in from the church stained glass window. She pondered all the stories told by her mistress Jane Hargreaves and Bryce Aiden Tyler, as well as Jane's Uncle Floyd's former business partner.

"Miss Jane," Silversmith started and then stopped. "Yes, Silversmith?" a tattered Jane replied.

Silversmith continued, "If the sign from that Spy ship... the raft that Mr. Tyler used to stay afloat... if that broke apart when the wave hit you... and if the men, as Magistrate Pinkney says, actually saw the fragments while anchored in the wine merchant's boat... then... then... Well, Miss Jane, how did you and Mr. Tyler survive?"

"Because, my dear Silversmith, of you," Jane smiled.

"I don't understand that," Billy Dawes, the carriage driver, offered.

Jane replied, "Fashion was of paramount importance to me because I had thought if I had no fortune to set my position in this society, then I must do so by fashion. When Mr. Tweedbottom insulted my silhouette, do you remember what you did?"

Silversmith thought, "I worked hard to repair your broken pannier, but when I couldn't, I looked for whalebone or baleen, but when we couldn't afford that,

Witherspoon and I crafted a substitute."

"Yes," Jane affirmed, "and you told me you invented something new."

"I recall," Silversmith replied, "Witherspoon took bark from the tree outside your Uncle Floyd's home and filled two sacs sewn stich-by-stich to mimic the shape of a pannier."

Jane smiled at Silversmith, "I wanted Mr. Tweedbottom to craft me a stunning dress so I could ring in the new year of 1777. I wanted to ignore the wars, which pepper us in these lands. I was superficial thinking I could not make any impact around me; I had made getting married my sole goal. This selfish passion in rushing God's timing blinded me to the true character of Mr. Tweedbottom."

"True character?" Silversmith asked.

Eliza Lucas explained, "Mr. Tweedbottom befriended Jane... to get close to the man who was hampering his slave trading business with Henry Mossop. He needed to kill Floyd Hargreaves."

"But," Jane continued, "the tree you used to fill my invented pannier..." Silversmith interrupted, "Witherspoon called it the *Quercus Suber* trees."

Bryce Aiden Tyler commented, "It is also known as the cork oak tree."

"Cork?" Billy Dawes asked, "The same stuff used to stop up wine bottles?"

"The very same," Magistrate Pinkney replied with a laugh. "Silversmith actually created huge pillows capable of floating in water."

Bryce Aiden Tyler added, "The bum roll you created had partially become detached from Miss Hargreaves' waist. I was able to use that and cling to Miss Hargreaves' corset strings, yet was confused when neither she nor I sank. Her skirts kept her lower body afloat. The bum roll, which lined her spine, kept her torso afloat. My other hand still grasped the cork-filled bag, which had ripped off from the lead rope I had tried to secure earlier. That and clinging to Jane kept me afloat, as well."

Jane's eyes moistened, "You saved my life, Silversmith. You saved Bryce and me both. We are both so grateful to you."

Bryce now nodded, "You may not have realized, Silversmith, but the bark from Floyd Hargreaves' trees are used to make cork. And cork was the same stuff I found aboard the wine merchant's boat, which we stuffed into bags and tied to a rope to save the survivors from the sinking ship."

Jane giggled, "The cork oak tree!"

Silversmith wondered aloud, "*Quercus Suber*... Cork oak!" She looked at Jane, "Witherspoon told me the previous owner of the property grew it as an experiment. I suppose that experiment was to see if they could make wine corks locally in these colonies."

Bryce Aiden Tyler said, "Your mistress Jane was unconscious when I found her. But because we were tied together, when the storm calmed, the natural motion of the waves eventually brought us back to shore, where Magistrate Karl Pinkney and Eliza Lucas found us."

"Imagine my surprise," Jane commented, "I awoke to being surrounded by water and Bryce, here kicking his legs to push us back to shore with the ebb and flow of the tides." She reached over and grasped both of Silversmith's hands, "You kept us afloat, Silversmith. You saved our lives."

Magistrate Pinkney interjected, "I thought they were lost at sea. I am certain planks of that ship shall be discovered from the old Swedish farming area of *Marrites Hoeck*... um... I mean, that Pirate Haven of Marcus Hook... to the Brandywine Shoal to Cape Henlopen of Lewes"

Eliza added, "The sailors on the docks said wreckage could be found near Long

Neck by the Indian River. It was a horrific disaster, yet it is miraculous only Mr. Tweedbottom seems to have perished."

Magistrate Pinkney nodded as he continued, "In a final attempt to search for Bryce Aiden Tyler, here, I sent the wine merchant's boat back out expecting to find a man's body, but to my surprise, the only body they found was that of Mr. Tweedbottom. Then, as they were returning to shore, one of my men spotted Bryce kicking in the water and pulled them both on board. They were not far from shore at all."

Eliza Lucas looked up at Magistrate Karl Pinkney and smiled, "Karl, you were so heroic to not have despaired of them. To keep hope burning brightly. I think I will make you a beautiful blue indigo coat, after all."

Turning to Jane and Bryce, Billy Dawes asked, "Aren't you tired after all that?"

"Thoroughly exhausted," Bryce replied, "But Jane... I mean, Miss Hargreaves, insisted on coming to the document signing no matter how she was attired."

7 CHAPTER 147: (JULY 4, 1776) Jane Wanted to See the Document Signed

In the church, the small tattered, exhausted group sat in the pews explaining events to Silversmith, Billy Dawes and Polly. Her newborn babe slept soundly.

Jane said, "I denied all rest. Freedom cares not for how I am attired. I simply had to come."

Magistrate Pinkney added, "I was uncertain about supporting such an event, however, after what I have discovered during this recent association with Mr. Bryce Aiden Tyler, here, I felt obligated to support these determined souls, Bryce and Miss Hargreaves."

"I thank you, Magistrate," Jane sincerely said to Magistrate Pinkney. "As this helps me successfully conclude my uncle's mission. I know who killed him and why. I know he was killed because he wanted to halt the mistreatment of the natives, as much as stop the kidnappings of colonial settlers to be sold as slaves. This document, I believe, addresses those points. I am sincerely obliged to you for helping me get here." Jane turned to Silversmith and asked, "Shall we depart to observe the congressional meeting?"

Silversmith clarified, "Miss Jane, they've locked the doors of the State House, so you cannot enter, but Mrs. Dunlap and the others will meet us afterwards."

Jane replied, "I don't mind getting a bit of rest here in this church. Besides, I am glad to be rid of the foul stench of greed, which fueled all this... this..."

"You mean," Silversmith offered, "Mr. Tweedbottom and the opera singer, Henry Mossop?" Jane replied, "And Marchioness de Waldegrave."

"Who?" Asked Silversmith.

Eliza Lucas answered, "You knew her as Lady Sarah Wilson, the woman who stole my mother's brooch." She took a breath and added, "She learned just enough refinement from her service to Queen Charlotte. Of course, she stole gowns and diamond jewelry from her Majesty. A necklace, I believe. She was caught and her punishment was to be sold as a slave here in the colonies. She escaped and ran to North Carolina, where she entered society under the name Marchioness de Waldegrave. She convinced people she was here by Queen Charlotte's request and posed as her sister."

"But, how would she survive? She had no money," Billy Dawes asked.

"Ah," Eliza Lucas replied, "She convinced her audience to donate funds to assist certain political causes she knew they already supported. She also stole, as she did from my father."

Magistrate Karl Pinkney added, "We discovered from our interrogation of Henry Mossop that Sarah Wilson, the name she was born with, formed an alliance with Mr. Mossop when she was low on funds. She took over a home because the owner decided to return to Europe. When Mr. Mossop proposed lucrative schemes, she became very cooperative. She simply needed to flatter men into opening their purses."

Bryce Aiden Tyler concluded, "But justice will be served. The magistrate has already dispatched his men to collect Miss Wilson."

"By now," Magistrate Karl Pinkney added, "she is secured in prison until I return."

Billy added, "Justice may take time, but 'tis satisfying when served."

Eliza offered, "And I took a tally of all the survivors from Henry Mossop's slave ship, which now is undoubtedly submerged under the ocean waters."

Silversmith asked, "The ship named the Spy?"

Eliza replied, "Yes. I asked each one rescued from the ship if any were lost at sea. All survived. The only fatality of the storm was that of Mr. Tweedbottom. "

Jane added, "If those hours unfolded as they should have, we would all have perished. However, God emboldened Mr. Tyler, here, and protected us all in the subsequent events which transpired. I believe this qualifies as a miracle. Our survival is against all the odds of nature. I have been thanking God since the Wine

Merchant's boat saw Mr. Tyler's splashes in the water, and rescued us."

Suddenly, deep robust sounds were heard from the rear of the church.

Every person sitting in the pews jumped: Magistrate Pinkney, Eliza Lucas, Jane Hargreaves, Bryce Aiden Tyler, Silversmith, Billy Dawes and Polly with her baby.

"What was that?" Polly gasped. Bryce replied, "An organ."

"I've never heard such sounds," Polly replied, "The music seems to be all around us, yet I see no person. You say this is from one instrument?"

Magistrate Pinkney said, "The concept has been around for some time. Panpipes use the same principle. Reed pipes and bellows were used to create a similar sound in the medieval regal organ of the sixteenth century."

"It's loud," Billy offered.

Then, the music stopped and a woman's giggle was heard from behind a wall. Then a man's laugh joined hers.

The small party looked at each other.

"I assumed the church was empty," Magistrate Pinkney said.

Eliza suggested, "Perhaps it is one of the keepers playing with the instrument."

A pastor emerged from a side door, startled to see people in the pews. He dropped a hymnbook, which he had been holding.

The slap of the leather bound book as it hit the floor reverberated against the stone walls. All remained silent.

Magistrate Pinkney was first to break the silence, "We thank you for allowing us in this House of God, sir."

The pastor replied, "I expected every person would be in that meeting. We were not expecting anybody to arrive until after it ended. They have been in that building since the second day of July, you know. Today, the fourth, I do hope they conclude. I was going to pray for God to guide them. Would you like to join me?"

Bryce Aiden Tyler stood up and said, "We would, sir." He gave a short bow to the ladies still sitting, and then strode to the man of the cloth, whispering once he had the old man's ear.

Those still remaining in the pews started to discuss the most proper way to join this pastor in prayer when they were so disheveled from their long ordeal.

Bryce quickly whispered to the pastor, "Could you marry me to that lady over there?"

"Eh?" The pastor replied, "Loud music stirs the soul, but takes a toll on the hearing."

Bryce repeated his request quickly.

"Oh! Tis an unexpected stipulation," the parson replied, "Which one?"

"The one least dressed for a wedding," Bryce shrugged as he turned his back to those sitting in the pew. "I've seen more of her in the last day than I believe is proper for an unmarried man to see of an unmarried lady, and I would like to right that..."

Looking over Bryce's shoulder, the pastor spotted Jane as her leg and a portion of her chemise popped out from under the blanket she grasped around her.

The pastor whispered in reply, "She looks as if she were caught in that storm... and that a number of people may have seen more of her than is considered appropriate in polite society."

"Indeed, Pastor, but I was a business partner to her uncle and have known her since she arrived to these colonies. I assure you, I have given the matter considerable thought for some time. We have sufficient witnesses for a wedding, do we not?"

The pastor evaluated Bryce before replying, "Sufficient witnesses, yes. I even have somebody who could sing hymns with a joyful voice."

"I believe I heard you and she demonstrating the organ earlier... from behind that wall. So, then..." Bryce prodded, glancing back at the others in the pew, realizing their conversations were ending and he needed to solidify clergy agreement to his proposal before he could return to the pews.

The pastor replied, "We are in the British Americas, now sir, so I will gladly marry you, provided..." He repeated sternly, "Provided that woman willingly agrees to your proper proposal of marriage. Our colonies may not be a country, but definitely this is not Europe. She has a say in matters such as these." The pastor took a step backwards and folded his arms.

With an impish smile, Bryce Aiden Tyler understood this clergy wished to see proof of his lasting intentions. Looking around the deserted church, Bryce saw something which caught his eye.

He walked quickly to the candles burning at the base of the alter and pulled one out of its holder, removing a small golden brass like ring around the base of the candle stick.

By now, the others had stopped talking and were watching Bryce with perplexed curiosity.

Bryce looked up and said a silent prayer, then walked to Jane and held out the ring, some two inches in diameter.

Bryce Aiden Tyler looked at Jane, took her hand and said, "Miss Hargreaves, I never want to experience the feeling of losing you ever again. Would you do me the honor of becoming my confidant, my companion, my cherished and forever adored wife?"

Surprised and shocked, Jane was speechless. Her hand pushed her hair from her brow.

Shocked, her eyes started to mist. All Jane could say was, "Mr. Tyler, I... I... Bryce... I... was not expecting this...I." She looked at her own disheveled clothes, still torn and dripping wet from her recent battles with the forces of the ocean.

"It is not your appearance I wish at my side," Bryce assured, "it is you... no matter the state of your dress."

Jane said nothing.

Bryce now, he felt his throat tighten with dryness while his palms moistened.

Bryce kneeled down on one knee in the aisle next to the pews and took Jane's hand. He slipped the two-inch wide candle base ring on her finger.

It fell off.

Then he slipped it on her thumb, but that too fell off, as well.

Jane leaned over and whispered to Bryce, "Would I be the best beloved of your heart always and forever?"

He smiled and replied softly, "Yes, Jane. I shall never be indifferent to you, nor allow another the opportunity to think they could steal the steady affections I hold for you. I have admired you from afar from the moment you arrived... from the first day I saw you... at..."

"At Uncle Floyd's home?" Jane prodded as she grasped the ring, much as a baby would grab a toy, since it was too large to fit any finger.

Bryce held Jane's hand in his. "Your character is just as noble and determined to enact justice as your uncle's," Bryce sighed as he looked deeply into Jane's eyes and clasped her hand to his chest. "At this very moment you are wondrously beautiful. No other could capture my heart as you have now or in days to come."

Jane looked around at the faces of the others. Polly and her baby, Magistrate Karl Pinkney, Eliza Lucas, Billy Dawes and of course Silversmith, who nodded and smiled with silent approval.

Then, Jane looked at the face of the curious Pastor who also appeared to be anxiously awaiting Jane's reply.

Bryce continued, "I realize normally such matches take proper courtship and months or even years of planning, and in some cases, if we had been betrothed for a time, we would use a bundling board.

"However, we are both mature and moral adults, Miss Hargreaves. We are in the House of God, amongst our most cherished and trusted friends. I implore you, Miss Hargreaves; we have just endured and survived the impossible. Please say yes, and marry me today."

"Now?" Jane asked, "You wish to marry now?"

"Yes," Bryce replied simply, "This very moment."

"Then," Jane started hesitantly, clearing her throat to enunciate each word carefully, "Yes, Bryce Aiden Tyler, I, Jane Hargreaves, would be overjoyed to be your wife..." Jane threw her arms around his neck.

Standing up, Bryce nodded to the pastor, who nodded in return with a smile.

8 CHAPTER 148: (JULY 4, 1776) The Second Proposal

Silversmith emerged from the side door of the vestibule of the church. She had done her best to comb Jane's hair and fitted Jane with the extra skirt she had retrieved earlier from the carriage. Jane still clung to the large ring Bryce had retrieved from the base of the candle stick.

Bryce gently approached Jane and said, "You are the epitome of the perfect bride." Jane blushed and looked down, smiling.

This was not her vision of her wedding day, but she could not have arranged such circumstances if she had tried... and she felt truly blessed to have captured the admiration of a man as gallant as Bryce Aiden Tyler.

She felt content and at peace.

Then, Bryce beckoned Silversmith to join him.

When she approached, Bryce asked Silversmith, "I know how much Jane relies on you. Would you, Silversmith, consider joining my household?"

"As a lady's maid?" Silversmith asked.

"Yes," Bryce replied, "at first. If you are willing, however, to take on more responsibilities, then I think an increase in your wages would be in order."

"Oh, Mr. Tyler, Sir…" Silversmith started, "But what of Mr. Floyd Hargreaves' butler?"

"Witherspoon?" Bryce Aiden Tyler asked.

Silversmith replied, "Pardon my boldness, sir. But it is not right that any member of Floyd Hargreaves' staff be unemployed because Miss Jane got married. What will happen to the current Hargreaves staff? Will they be without wages?"

Bryce smiled and replied, "I admire your concern, Silversmith. I have already asked Witherspoon to consider my offer, and the others in Floyd's employ were occasional workers, but they are welcomed to continue working in my household. Witherspoon told me he could not answer me because he promised to wait until Miss Hargreaves returned from her mission. I have noted that Witherspoon has also befriended a cook at the grand estate, and I am considering extending an offer to her, as well. "

Silversmith replied, "May I be bold once again, sir? I wish to ask about Mr. Dawes, there. Miss Jane has just extended an invitation to him, and he accepted. He holds great intelligence, sir. He even shared an idea about setting up roads and stops to improve parcel delivery services. I suggested he ask Miss Susanna Wright to foster an introduction to Mr. Benjamin Franklin to discuss opportunities."

Bryce smiled and replied, "I could use an expert driver, as well as a creative man of ideas. Let us see how we may put his sound concepts into practice. Consider your Billy Dawes invited to join my household, as well, Silversmith. Now, what say you?"

"In that case," Silversmith replied, "I would be honored to accept, and join your household staff, Mr. Tyler, sir."

The pastor approached Bryce Aiden Tyler and asked, "Shall we begin?"

Bryce looked to Silversmith, "Should we start now or wait until the meeting adjourns and the others convene with us?"

Silversmith stepped quietly to Polly, then to Jane. She soon returned and said, "The ladies would like to wait until the others arrive to witness the ceremony. They are but a ten minute walk from here."

The pastor replied, "Lovely. Therefore, I shall use that time to confer with my singer to select appropriate hymns."

9 CHAPTER 149: (JULY 4, 1776)
The Meeting Adjourns

"Hurry," Mrs. Dunlap beckoned to her friends as the other meeting attendees streamed around them toward the exits like grains of sand in an hourglass.

Mrs. Dunlap continued to speak loudly over the buzz of the crowds, "It took them far too long to unbolt those doors. We must get to the carriage as I've got to have Mr. Dunlap print out a copy of the broadside for John Hancock to authenticate."

"But what of Polly?" Susanna Wright asked as Eunice and TallMan were trying to push their way through the crowds to meet with Mrs. Dunlap and Susanna.

"Yes! And Jane, as well. We must get her word." Mrs. Dunlap enthused as she stood up on the balls of her feet to see over the crowd.

When TallMan reached them, Mrs. Dunlap asked him, "TallMan, could you look over the heads of these people and see if Mr. Dawes is at the carriage?"

TallMan looked in the direction of the carriages, turned back to Mrs. Dunlap leaning down a bit and replied, "I do not see anybody at the carriage."

"Then, they are at the church," Eunice offered. "It is but a ten minute walk. Shall we?"

The small party started to march briskly. Susanna suddenly stepped a few feet in front of them and then stopped, holding her hands out.

"I must tell you all something," Susanna started, "I have been remiss to not mention it earlier..."

For a brief moment, the crowds cleared as carriages were leaving and Mrs. Dunlap announced, "I say! Is that my carriage?"

Mrs. Dunlap clarified, "Susanna, dear, we haven't time for dramatics. You heard the man inside. They want all the signatures within a fortnight, but with the amount of changes, we'll be lucky to get them to sign it by... by... the first Friday in August."

"You need to know," Susanna started again as the crowds pushed forward, bumping Susanna.

Without allowing Susanna to finish, Mrs. Dunlap marched smartly in the direction of the parked carriages.

She explained to TallMan, "I had loaned it to some travelers last night when they did not have room at the inn."

TallMan looking in the direction asked, "Which is it?" and Mrs. Dunlap described it.

TallMan shared, "There appear to be people inside. One man is talking to others and... Oh. He dropped his bag and spilled the contents..."

Then Susanna interjected, "That's the man from the docks last night. The one who asked for directions to the inn."

Mrs. Dunlap recognized him and said, "That is the very same fellow to whom I loaned my carriage... Was he at the meeting? Onward, team." Mrs. Dunlap raised an arm and led the group as they swiftly approached her carriage.

But TallMan stopped her, "Mrs. Dunlap. The man to whom Susanna dropped the bottle of ink is over there. He beckons us."

"The village doctor?" Susanna asked.

Just then, the bearded village doctor hurriedly approached; "Oh!" he said breathlessly, "I am so pleased I caught up with you."

"Yes?" Mrs. Dunlap asked impatiently as she glanced over to her carriage where the man both Susanna and she recognized was collecting the contents of his bag.

The doctor explained, "Miss Wright, that is your name, is it not?"

"I don't recall having met you, Sir," Susanna replied.

The doctor peered over his spectacles and clarified, "Oh, I do not know you, but my patient does. He saw you when you stood up with the ink. That is why I offered to catch it. At his behest."

"Who is your patient, Doctor?" Susanna inquired.

The doctor beckoned the group to follow him, "I think he said he recognized you, Sir, as well." TallMan looked around him, "Do you refer to me? I do not know anybody in attendance, here." Curiosity gripped the tiny party and they followed the doctor to a bench on which this man sat. When he looked up, Susanna cried, "Button Gwinette?"

He smiled, "My leg is damaged, so I could not rise to sign the document when called and had to wait until a path was cleared for me and even then, I needed aid to get up there. From the balcony, all you would have seen was a cluster of men approaching John Hancock."

Susanna relieved, shared, "I was feeling guilty that I had been remiss in my duties to bring you, here."

The doctor interjected, "Mr. Gwinette here insisted I accompany him to this signing."

Button explained, "After a red coat found the doctor, he took me in, but was so preoccupied with my injuries, that he did not have time to return to the docks when summoned. I begged him to take his horse and ride me here, as I wanted to keep my word for representing Georgia. And the good doctor obliged me."

TallMan smiled, "I thought I recognized you. I could not recall where I had seen you before, as I only saw the top of your head from the balcony above. Now I recall you visited me with Farmer in the forest. You helped him fill water jugs for meetings... the very same meetings, which resulted in the document being signed today."

Button smiled as he replied, "I did not wish to get involved, yet now I am one representative for Georgia. It is good to see you, my friend."

Mrs. Dunlap smiled, "Your name is Button? Button Gwinette?"

"Yes, and you are?" Button asked.

All aflutter, Mrs. Dunlap replied, "My name is Mrs. Dunlap." She wiggled her fingers in the air as she turned to Susanna, "Go fetch my carriage immediately. We must bring this wounded man to the church to meet... the rest of our friends. Hurry!"

Susanna ran off in the direction of Mrs. Dunlap's carriage

.

10 CHAPTER 150: (JULY 4, 1776) Getting the Carriage...

Mrs. Dunlap dispatched Susanna Wright to fetch her carriage to help the wounded Button Gwinette get to the church to meet the others.

Mrs. Dunlap turned to Button and smiled, "We'll have proper transportation for you shortly, Mr. Gwinette."

Button smiled appreciatively. He thought of all he had been through.

He wondered if his efforts to struggle to stay alive, to take a risk, to speak up when he should have been silent, to grasp the wisps of hope as if it were rope which would support him as he pulled in his dreams... was it worth it?

Button did it for his unborn child and beloved wife Polly, who hopefully had escaped...

Yet. Button did not know for certain if his wife was safe or even still alive. He closed his eyes for a moment, then he smiled again at Mrs. Dunlap, but every effort he made filled him with pain.

Susanna ran to the lot where all the carriages stood with their drivers and horses.

This was the carriage, which Mrs. Dunlap had loaned the night before to some newly docked sailors and their party.

There was no room at the inn, in which she had lodged, and she felt guilty leaving them without a mode of transport to another lodging option.

As she tried to catch her breath, Susanna noticed the man was indeed the sailor she had met at the docks before the others had even boarded the Spy ship.

He was picking up the contents of his spilt sac. He looked up and smiled as he recognized her. "Hello, again," he grinned.

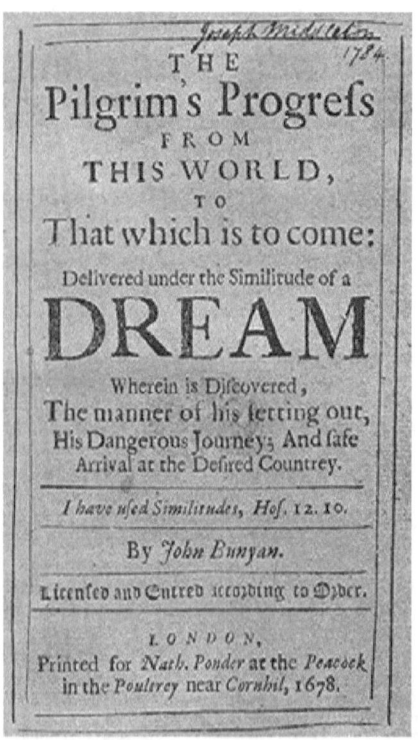

His travelling companions noted the lingering gaze his sailor bestowed upon Susanna as he stood there clutching a book.

Susanna looked down at the book he held. "Is that **'Pilgrim's Progress from this World to That Which is to Come'?"**

One mariner nudged him and beckoned to the other fellows to leave this sailor be...alone with Susanna, the object of his attentions.

The sailor's companion announced, "We'll be at the pub. Will you be at the church?"

The mariner replied to his cohorts, "I'll find you at the pub, then."

"That book, Sir..." Susanna started.

"Yes?" The sailor replied as his companions left.

Susanna stuttered and replied, "It is by John Bunyan. Written in 1678. Why is a sailor carrying a century old book?"

"It's reprinted from the original," he explained as he picked up a scarf and shoved it into his bag.

Susanna noticing the mariner's travelling companions had departed leaned in and whispered, "Don't all sailors make haste to the local pub when in port? Why do your companions think you should be at a church?"

"Oh!" The mariner commented as he picked up another book, which had fallen from his bag, "I was conscripted into the King Georgie's navy a while back. The others enjoy drink. I enjoy reading," he winked at her, "The stories allow me to entertain the other fellows during long days at sea."

"So, you share your books?"

"Oh, they would borrow them if they could read," the sailor explained. "I had been educated before getting conscripted, so I either read to them or summarize the story to entertain them."

Susanna was speechless.

He gave a short bow and introduced himself as, "Scriobhai at your service." He placed a copy of another book titled **Magnalia Christi Americana** by that Preacher Cotton Mather, into his bag.

Susanna paused, recognizing the title. She wondered if this sailor, who introduced himself as Scriobhai, would agree with Mr. Cotton Mather's views denouncing slavery. Perhaps she could assume he did.

Susanna asked, "Scriobhai? Is that not the word for 'scribe' in Gaelic?"

The sailor laughed. "You are the first person I have met who knew that fact before I disclosed it. A reader, eh?"

Susanna asked, "How did you discern I had read it and not that I had lived in Ireland myself?"

"Tis nothing, Miss..." Scriobhai replied.

"Please. Do tell me as I admire your deductive reasoning, for it is... honestly... accurate," Susanna persisted.

"As you wish," the sailor started. "You knew its meaning, yet did not pronounce it properly. I reasoned you read the knowledge and can read some Gaelic passages, yet may not have encountered a native speaker so you could not have lived there. Your mispronunciation tells me you enjoy reading quite a bit. Do you?"

"I do, quite..." Susanna replied as she tried to peek into his bag to see other books, which may give insight into his personality. "But, I approach you this moment about another matter. I have been asked to fetch the carriage for Mrs. Dunlap over there," Susanna pointed to where Mrs. Dunlap and the others waited, "You see, Mr. Scriobhai..."

He interrupted her, "Please call me Patrick. Unusual to be so informal, I know, but I feel we will become very good friends..."

"This is indeed highly unusual, Mr. Scriobhai..." Susanna gasped, unable to clarify her thoughts about her immediate task.

"Would you feel better calling me Patrick if you knew that 'Scriobhai' was given to me when I docked for some time in Ireland? It is not my family name. At sea, oft times, one gets a new name and that was assigned because I could read and write. Not all mariners were so blessed."

Taken aback, Susanna asked, "Was the name Patrick also given to you by your mariner companions?"

"Nay," Patrick smiled, "It is merely a good name to call me. One most can pronounce."

"So, you are not Irish?" Susanna asked, "Yet have a Gaelic or Irish name?"

Patrick responded with a question of his own, "And your name is?"

"Oh, Right. Susanna Wright," she replied.

"Are you Miss Right or simply Susanna Wright?" Patrick asked.

"Susanna, then," Susanna conceded,

"If you choose to be informal with me, I shall return the offer of friendship, as I also think we might become good friends."

Patrick commented, "Susanna. Suzey. Beautiful name. Poetic it is. It evokes

images of graceful lilies growing on rolling grassy knolls."

Susanna Wright's hand clutched her bosom as she gasped, "Some say Susanna does mean lily... You are indeed well read, sir."

Patrick added, "In one port, I met a man who captured the sentiments of that exquisite flower. I urged him to one day collect all his works and create a volume to distribute at bookshops. He said he must wait a few more years until he has written enough poems to publish a book. He is barely twenty years today and may need to experience life a few more years before he has sufficient inspiration for poetry."

"Indeed?" Susanna declared.

Patrick replied, "This fellow's words capture the imagery of a fragile pure flower. Although without flaw, the lily beckons for love and protection as it has no thorns to defend itself, yet earnestly changes even the most defiled landscape with its innocent beauty."

"That is quite presumptuous," Susanna retorted. "I think lilies could fight if need be."

Patrick took a step closer to Susanna and she did not step back, but gazed into his eyes. It appeared as if all other sounds had faded in volume.

No longer could she detect the wooden carriage wheels of other carriages departing, grinding against the stony pebbles on the ground.

No longer could she hear the grunts of horses or servants helping their passengers into their vehicles.

No longer could she discern people greeting each other and commenting about the recent events, which had just occurred inside the State House.

She could only detect a soft breeze against her cheek, the effervescent song of a chirping bird overhead, her own breath and the deep resonating voice of this mariner, Patrick Scriobhai, which was not even his birth given name.

Patrick leaned in and spoke softly so only she could hear, "If I recall, he wrote: *The modest Rose puts forth a thorn, The humble sheep a threat'ning horn: While the Lily white shall in love delight, Nor a thorn nor a threat stain her beauty bright.*"

He then took a step back and adjusted his bag on his shoulder. Patrick spoke now in louder more conversational tones, "If you enjoy poetry, I predict this fellow's words will touch the hearts of lovers for decades once he can pen more poems. When he is older, should he produce a book of poetry, I would suggest you procure it for your enjoyment. His name is William Blake. I predict England would be proud to call such a talented fellow a citizen of the Crown."

"I will note that name, thank you, Patrick," Susanna said quietly.

Patrick replied, "I'm glad there was no room at the first inn, as I was able to attend this meeting where everybody in town seemed to be."

"I was in the very same meeting. At the State House," Susanna replied, and then frowned, "But the carriage, Patrick. It must be returned to Mrs. Dunlap forthwith."

He paused a moment, then Patrick shared, "Does Mrs. Dunlap require the carriage this very moment? I was quite enjoying our conversation, Suzey. Susanna..."

Susanna Wright, now regaining her composure replied, "Mrs. Dunlap sent me to fetch the carriage, as it is needed to transport a wounded man to the church."

"I know that church," Patrick replied as he repositioned the bag on his shoulder.

"Oh, so you know where the church lays?" Susanna clarified as she peeked into his bag and now saw a copy of the Bible.

Patrick explained as he shoved some clothing into his bag, covering the Holy Book, "Because you directed me to the inn, I met your friend Mrs. Dunlap, who showed an act of kindness to us newly arrived strangers, by lending her carriage to us."

He hoisted his bag back onto his shoulder, as he explained, "One event opens the door to the next surprise in our lives. 'Tis up to each one of us to walk through that door and that is what I did. You see, we needed to deliver one of our sea faring passengers to that very same church. Because we transported our passenger in good condition, the Pastor thanked us by providing hot stew, fresh bread, and warm dry beds for us all. Last night, I slept in a dry bed because of you, Suzey Wright."

Susanna blushed, something she rarely did, and replied, "Suzey? Oh my. Yes. Well, I suppose we all play a small part in God's plan, then," Susanna commented, "But although I was sent to secure this carriage, I confess I do not know how to manage more than one horse... and this has two..."

Repositioning his sac, Patrick replied, "While my fellow mariners are happily occupied in the local pub, please allow me to be your driver." He bowed again.

"Very well," Susanna said as she accepted his extended hand to board Mrs. Dunlap's carriage. Pleased, Patrick tossed his bag with ease onto the roof of the carriage behind the driver's bench.

Before Patrick ascended the side of the carriage, he leaned in and said to Susanna, "I do hope we may find time to learn of other books we both might enjoy. Yes. I saw you spying my titles in my bag..." He smiled and moved away before Susanna had time to reply.

Susanna smiled and positioned herself with very straight posture inside the carriage, grinning as Patrick closed the door.

Then, inside, as the carriage bounced under the weight of Patrick bounding up to grab the reins, Susanna leaned back and quickly muttered to herself, "Huh. Interesting."

Patrick climbed up to the driver's seat and snapped the reins. They quickly made their way to the area where Button Gwinette, the doctor, TallMan, Eunice, and Mrs. Dunlap awaited.

The doctor assisted Button and his wounded leg into the carriage.

Susanna's new friend, Patrick, gingerly provided his arm as a guide for Mrs. Dunlap to enter the carriage. Mrs. Dunlap leaned out and spoke to the doctor, "Won't you join us, doctor?"

TallMan bounded up to the driver's perch and smiled at the sailor, Patrick, who evaluated TallMan's stature cautiously determining if this was friend or foe.

"I thank you, Madame," he replied, "But I have other matters to attend to before returning home to my wife and children. My carriage awaits on the other side of the State Building. Mr. Gwinette will need to keep his leg extended. I believe your compartment is full."

The doctor assisted TallMan's mother, Eunice, into the compartment without a word.

"I thank you," Button shouted out, "For your attention during the dark night and for delivering me to the State House meeting of Congress."

"I am pleased you are feeling better, sir," the doctor replied, "I bid you all a very fare well. When you return home, do see your local doctor. Else, send me word and I will endeavor to assist you to health."

The village doctor straightened his spectacles, turned on his heels and, with a rapid stride, walked away.

11 What Just Happened?

The tiny accomplished group were surprised when the Magistrate welcomed them inside the church. Then, we learned about what happened aboard the SPY mere hours earlier during a huge storm on July 3rd 1776 and how Jane's life hung precariously as she fell overboard.

When Bryce Aiden Tyler sought to commandeer a wine merchant's vessel, he also succumbed to the storm and plunged into the cold foreboding waters. The men with him searched until early morning to no avail. Yet, at the church, a tale of survival gingerly unfolds and it is revealed that those who were diligent in finding solutions actually may have inadvertently saved a life. Silversmith is stunned.

The women were all driven by different motives yet a common goal to participate in witnessing the signing of the Document, the Declaration of Independence! Polly yearned for the safety of her husband and worried about her unborn child.

Jane earnestly sought justice to discover the reason for her uncle Floyd's death. Eunice wanted her own childhood enslavement and subsequent adoption which led to TallMan's medicinal education to help others. Mrs. Dunlap, the printer's wife, earnestly wanted to see a document which would make a difference and more...

All these various motives drove each of the women to participate in the dissemination of the Declaration. And now, the group has disbanded yet there are more surprises when they gather at the carriage.

12 Did You Know...

One of the signers of the *Declaration of Independence*, William Whipple, felt he could not fight for his own liberties and freedom from the oppression of the British Crown while owning a slave himself. He did not want to be a hypocrite. William Whipple did want to set the example for others to free their own slaves.

William Whipple showed his resolute determination to fight for freedom for all people. To prove that he believed in freedom for all people, William Whipple freed his slave who was named Prince Whipple.

In the short time this *Firebrand* story takes place (1776) and during the Revolutionary War (April 19, 1775 – September 3, 1783), messages were embedded in between the lines of text of regular hand-written letters. Those hidden lines were written in invisible ink. This ink could have been a mix of ferrous (iron- based) sulfate and water.

This invisible ink was made visible by the heat of a candle flame, or by washing the letter with a chemical substance reagent such as sodium carbonate, which would reveal the letter's hidden contents. This practice may have been the origin of the phrase "read between the lines", which means that there is another meaning which is not obvious.

Today, you can make "invisible ink" with baking soda and water. You can also use lemon juice.

Some say that Washington advised secret spies to write hidden messages on the pages of common items such as almanacs, books, and pamphlets.

Pliny the Elder, a Roman naturalist, used milk of the *tithymalus* plant (goat lettuce). The invisible ink would become visible when ashes were sprinkled on it. Philo of Byzantium c. 280-220 B.C. in Alexandria used crushed gallnuts dissolved in water.

To reveal the "ink", dab it with a sponge soaked in *virrol* (ferrous sulfate). Also dry heat, such as sunshine for a couple days or a low-grade oven for a few moments may "bake" the ink and make it visible..

"The die is cast... it seems to me the Sword is now our only, yet dreadful, alternative...."– *Abigail Adams, wife of John Adams, in a letter to a friend in February 1775*

The Hurricane of Independence was a real-life storm which occurred on September 2, 1775. David M. Ludlum dubbed the storm the *"Independence Hurricane of 1775"* because it struck North Carolina on the 2nd of September, "just as the opening maneuvers of the War of Independence were in progress."

This storm devastated the Colony of Newfoundland, killing an estimated 4,000 sailors from England and Ireland, making it one of the deadliest Atlantic hurricanes of all time with surges up to 30 feet.

Some estimate the winds gusted to 140 miles per hour or 220 kilometers per hour. This impacted Newfoundland, Virginia and North Carolina. The Virginia Gazette reported, *"the corn laid almost level with the ground, and fodder destroyed; many ships and other vessels drove ashore and were damaged, at Norfolk, Hampton, and York."*

Another source described the storm: "*...At Placentia, which stood directly in the path of the storm, many survived only by scrambling into the rafters of their homes as the wind drove flood-waters three and four feet deep through the town...*" Olaf Uwe Janzen, "Newfoundland and British Maritime Strategy during the American Revolution" (Unpublished PhD thesis, Queen's University, 1983), 145.

In addition to damage on land, the Royal Navy lost two schooners which were enforcing the British fishing along the Grand Banks of Newfoundland.

A Poem of that time recited by sailors is titled "Mariner's Poem", which was cited on p.86 in R. Inwards, *Weather Lore* (London, 1898)

June — too soon;
July — stand by;
August — look out, you must;
September — remember;
October — all over.

In real-life history, the very first German translation of the *Declaration of Independence* was printed on Tuesday, July 9, 1776 on the front page of *Pennsylvanischer Staatsbote* newspaper, managed by Henrich Millers. A German translation was also published as a broadside , by Millers' junior colleagues Melchior Steiner and Carl Cist.

Also on July 9th, 1776, George Washington read a copy (in English) to his New York City troops after the President of the Congress, John Hancock, sent Washington a broadside. At the time, thousands of foreboding British troops were on ships in the harbor nearby.

The effect the words of the *Declaration of Independence* had served to inspire the locals. They removed all symbols of British royalty. A statue of King George sitting authoritatively on a horse was torn down and made into musket-balls (bullets) to fight the British red-coats. The Colonists were determined to fight regardless of the odds against them.

Maier, Pualine, "American Scripture", p156-157

Symbolism

It was in 1774 that Thomas introduced the device, borrowed from the *Constitutional Courant* of 1765, which represented a snake divided into nine parts, one part denoting New England, and each of the remaining parts denoting the other colonies — the Immortal Thirteen in all. Over this, in large letters, extending the entire width of the page, was the motto, "JOIN OR DIE." This device had created a sensation in the streets of New York nine years previously. It increased the excitement in 1774.

Isaiah Thomas, editor of newspaper "The Spy" supported the Revolution.

Image 1- Excerpt from the book Journalism in the United States, from 1690-1872 By Frederic Hudson..This work is in the public domain in the United States of America, and possibly other nations. Within the United States, you may freely copy and distribute this work, as no entity (individual or corporate) has a copyright on the body of the work.

Spy Ship

The Spy ship mentioned in this story is fictitious, but there was a ship named Spy, which had been purchased for 200 pounds at Stonington. It was a schooner which could hold about 50 tons. It had formerly been called the "Britannia", which was deemed inappropriate for a ship in the new Colonial Navy fighting the British. Her purpose was to gather intelligence. Robert Niles became the captain of the newly named Spy vessel. He was later replaced by Samuel Niles.

In the end two vessels were obtained, one chartered and the other purchased. These two vessels, the first of the Connecticut navy, were the Minerva and the Spy.

Image 2 New England Magazine, Volume 35, September 1906–February 1907, : The Connecticut Navy of the American Revolution by By CHARLES OSCAR PAULLIN, PH. D., Page 715

By October 1775, the Spy was deemed seaworthy. Around July 1776, (between 1775-1779) Mr.Nathanial Shaw Jr. was appointed an "Agent for the Colony" to manage naval supplies and also arrange a process to provide health-care for sick seamen. Here is how the duties of his role were clarified, "...*the purpose of naval supplies and for taking care of such sick seamen as may be sent on shore to his care.*"

Mr. Shaw was chosen because of his good social reputation. He also had experience importing goods and he lived in Boston, a strategic location. He was close to George Washington and other leaders of the American Revolution. One local newspaper described an event this way: "*A great wedding dance took place at New London at the house of Nathaniel Shaw, Esq., June 12, 1769, the day after the marriage of his son Daniel Shaw and Grace Coit. 92 gentlemen and ladies attended, and danced 92 jigs, 52 contra-dances, 45 minuets, and 17 horn-pipes, and retired 45 minutes past midnight.*"

Underwater Vessel

Samuel Elliot held the same position as Mr. Shaw, but Mr. Elliot lived in Connecticut. Governor Jonathan Trumbull consulted with Mr. Elliot to improve the Connecticut navy. As a result of this search for improvements, they communicated with David Bushnell, a graduate of Yale in the class of 1775, who had an invention for a submersible vessels which could fight the enemy underwater. David Bushnell proposed the idea to blow up ships in February 1776. He was given £60 to execute this idea. The vessel was called "American Turtle", a tortoise-shaped diving-boat which could be propelled from under water. The vessel could supply air to an operator for 30 minutes. This did not prove to be successful.

Spy in Europe

The Connecticut navy was called upon to stop the illegal and illicit trafficking enacted by unprincipled Tories and other British traders in Connecticut, Massachusetts, Long Island and New York and as far away as the Azores and the West Indies..

In June and July of 1778, ships transported Indigo to Nantes, France expecting to trade it for clothing, but a storm demasted the ship.

The Spy replaced the damaged ship and made the voyage to France. The Spy was the only vessel which visited a European port successfully.

The vessels of the Connecticut navy with the approximate periods of their services were as follows: brigantine Minerva, 1775; schooner Spy, 1775-1778; ship Defence, 1776-1779; ship Oliver Cromwell, 1776-1779; galleys Crane and Whiting, 1776; galley Shark, 1776-1777; schooner Schuyler, 1777; and sloop Guilford, 1779. A list of vessels in the Connecticut navy, that contains several additional names, has been compiled.

....

By all odds the chiefest vessels of the Connecticut navy were the Spy, Defence, and Oliver Cromwell. Each belonged to the navy for some three years and saw considerable service.

Image 3 New England Magazine, Volume 35, September 1906–February 1907, : The Connecticut Navy of the American Revolution by By CHARLES OSCAR PAULLIN, PH. D., Page 720

The Spy in real-life proved to be a very useful vessel.

The first prize of a Connecticut state vessel was captured by the tiny schooner Spy, which made her first cruise in October, 1775. Early in that month she re-captured and brought into New London a large ship containing eight thousand bushels of wheat. The Spy was chiefly useful in watching the enemy and giving notice of his movements to the government and to the shipping of the state.

Image 4 New England Magazine, Volume 35, September 1906–February 1907, : The Connecticut Navy of the American Revolution by By CHARLES OSCAR PAULLIN, PH. D., Page 721

The Spy was very small so could evade the enemy easily. She carried about 30 men and could seek refuge in shallow harbors and rivers where larger ships could not venture.

The crew of the Spy was given very specific orders.

On July 6, 1776, the following instructions were issued by Governor Trumbull and the Connecticut Council of Safety to Captain Robert Niles "of the Colony armed Schooner Spy": "You are hereby instructed carefully and diligently to attend the duty of your station and department; to keep a careful watch and lookout for any and every hostile ship or vessel which may be hovering about our coasts, take any that you can, give every signal and intelligence of and concerning them in your power; and for the advantage of the trade and friends of the country, you are also to take care and prevent, as far as lies in your power, any smuggling trade and clandestine management contrary to the laws and embargo of this Colony, and any of the prohibitions of the honourable Continental Congress; for which, and every faithful exertion for the good of the Colonies and the support of the laws, this shall be your sufficient warrant."

Image 5 New England Magazine, Volume 35, September 1906–February 1907, : The Connecticut Navy of the American Revolution by By CHARLES OSCAR PAULLIN, PH. D., Page 721

The Spy captured ships bearing cargoes of food. One example was:

fifty-nine hogsheads of rum and eight barrels of sugar; and the ship Hope laden with 250 hogsheads of Sugar, thirty-two puncheons of rum, and some molasses and coffee

The Connecticut schooner, Spy, along with other ships, was selected to execute an important mission. The Spy, captained by Robert Niles, carried news and copies of the Congressionally ratified French-United States treaty of February 1778. Niles was the first to reach France with the important message. Upon his return, the Spy was captured by the British, as was Niles. Captain Niles escaped twice, returning to Connecticut about a year after he first sailed to France.

The July 1779 Connecticut Council of Safety reports: *"Captain Niles came in, having arrived home last Saturday after having been twice captured, etc.—gave an account of his voyage, etc.—arrived at Paris twenty-seven days after he sailed, which was June, 1778, and delivered his mail to Dr. Franklin, containing the ratification by Congress of the Treaty with France, being the first account he had received of that event, which was greatly satisfactory to him and the French minister and nation in general, etc."*

The name "Spy" was used on another ship later. In a document published in 1799 titled "List of Ships lost, taken or destroyed from the Enemy, from January to June", there were two references to ships, one in 1794 (a captured French ship renamed "Spy") and it was listed again in 1795.

A

LIST OF SHIPS

LOST, TAKEN, OR DESTROYED,

FROM

THE ENEMY,

SINCE

THE COMMENCEMENT OF THE WAR.

[Thofe to which a • is prefixed are now in the Britifh Navy.]

† La Prompt, 20 guns, was the firft fhip launched by the French Republic, and the firft fhip taken of 20 guns.

THE NAVAL CHRONICLE.

VOL.   *I.*

FROM JANUARY TO JUNE.

MDCCXCIX.

FRENCH SHIPS LOST, TAKEN, OR DESTROYED, SINCE THE COMMENCEMENT OF THE WAR.

1794.

Ship	Guns	Ref	Remarks
La Moselle, H. A. Bennett	20	T.1793	Taken at Toulon after the Evacuation, January 7. (Since retaken)
Convert, J. Lawford, (form. Inconft.)	36	T.1793	Lost on the Grand Caymanes, February. Crew faved
Spitfire, (fch) T. W. Rich	8	P.1793	Overfet off St. Domingo, February. Crew loft
Arcto, R. M. Sutton	64	1793	Loft off Corfica. Suppofed to be blown up by Accident, with the Crew
Caftor, T. Troubridge	32	1793	Taken off Cape Clear, May 9, re-taken May
Alert, C. Smyth	18	1793	By L'Unite of 40 Guns, off the Coaft of Ireland, May. Since loft
L'Efpion (Sp) W. H. Kirtoe	18	P.1793	By Three French Frigates,—Retaken, now named Spy
Speedy (Sp) G. Eyre (retaken)	14	1793	Taken off Nice, June
La Profelyte	24	T.1793	A Floating-Battery, and funk off Baftia by the Fire of the French Batteries
Rofe, M. Scott	28	1793	Loft on Rocky Point, Jamaica, June 28. Crew faved
Ranger (Cut) Lieut. Cotgrave	14	P.1793	Taken off Breft, June.—Retaken
Hound, R. Piercy	16	1793	By La Seine and Galatea, coming from the Weft Indies, July 14
Scout, C. Robinfon	16	1793	By Two French Frigates, off Cape Bona, Auguft. (Since loft)
L'Impetueux	74	T.1793	Burnt by Accident in Portfmouth Harbour, Auguft 29. Crew faved
Alexander, Rear-Adm. R. R. Bligh	74	1793	Taken off Scilly, Nov. 6, by Five Seventy-Fours & Three Frigates. Retaken
Placentia (Sp.) Lieut. A. Sheppard		1793	Loft at Newfoundland. Crew faved
L'Actif, F. Jn. Harvey	16	T.1793	Foundered off Bermuda, November 26. Crew faved
Daphne, W. E. Cracraft	20	1773	Taken by Two French Men of War.—Retaken Dec. 28, 1797

1795.

Ship	Guns	Remarks
Neptune	80	Cut away in the Bay of Hodierne, January
Le Scipion	80	Foundered in a Gale of Wind, January
Le Neaf Thermidor	80	
La Superbe	74	
Le Dumas	20	By Bellona, G. Wilfon, and Alarm, J. Carpenter, January 5
La Duquefne	44	By the Bellona, G. Wilfon, in the Weft Indies, January
La Pique (fince loft)	38	By the Blanche, R. Faulknor, in the Weft Indies, January 6
L'Efperance	22	By the Argonaut, J. Ball, on the Coaft of America, Jan. 8
La Courteufe (fch)	12	By the Pomone, Sir J. B. Warren, off the Ifle of Groaix, February
Rejoin (a b)	12	By the Thalia, R. Grindall, February
L'Efpion (now the Spy)	18	By the Lively, Geo. Burlton, off Breft, March 2
La Tourterelle	30	By the Lively, G. Burlton, 11 Leagues from Ufhant, March 13
Ca Ira	80	By the Fleet under Vice-Admiral W. Hotham, off Genoa, March 14

Image 6 Excerpt from pages of the List of French Ships Lost Taken... since the start of the war

13 Vocabulary

In the early 1770s, before the colonies united into the United States of America, some words and terms were used, which may be explained in this section.

Bumroll or **Rump-pad**- This was an undergarment usually stuffed with cork or other firm yet light-weight stuffing inside a linen or cotton case and tied around the waist. This would be over the pannier and petticoat, but under the outer skirt. Sometimes ladies would wear this instead of a pannier, but several wore it on top of a pannier.

Chemise - This is sometimes called a "shift" and modern terms would be "slip".

This was a sheath of fabric made of cotton or linen or silk. It was the garment which touched the skin and served as the foundation for all the other garments layered on top. It extended from the knees to the calf area of your leg. Both men and women wore a shift. A woman must never be seen in just a chemise as she would be considered "un-clothed". Only her ladies maid or her husband could see her in such a state.

Condemneth (p7) This is an old fashioned way of saying you blame or condemn a person. It is as if it were saying "he who blames the good" or "He who blames or frames an innocent person for a crime they never committed...."

Jetsamed (p9)...Pushing away. The Jetsam is a part of a ship, or the cargo on the ship or any equipment used to operate the ship which is heaved overboard to lighten the load during a time when the ship is in trouble and must shed weight so it can remain afloat.

Often, that which was heaved overboard either sinks or is washed ashore. In the 1560's the word "*Jottsome*" was an act of throwing goods overboard to lighten a ship. The old French word is "*getaison* ". A modern version of the word is "Jettison". In the 1590's the word "Flotsam" was used as "goods thrown away overboard"

Justifieth (p7) This is an old fashioned way of saying 'he who makes an excuse for bad behavior..."

Pannier- Some may call this undergarment a "hoop skirt". Pannier comes from the French word for "basket" and resembled a bird cage shape. This was a garment which was used underneath the outer skirt to provide volume. Around the 1720's large dome-shaped skirts were considered fashionable. The larger your "hips" meant you could afford more fabric of the skirt to cover it, which implied you had sufficient wealth to spend on extra fabric. By the 1730's the pannier became a rounded oval shape. By 1745, it became wide, oblong at the hips, and flat on the front and rear of the skirt. Around 1770, a rounded hoop-skirt was coming into fashion. The underskirt, Pannier, held its shape by using a frame of wood, whalebone, reeds, or anything stiff which could support the weight of petticoats and an over-skirt.

Instead of a "handbag" or "purse", side slits allowed a woman to reach into a **pocket**, which was a pouch connected to a waistband. The wide hip design of the pannier-cage allowed for large pockets which could hold a smaller purse of heavy coins, keys, mirror, or anything else. Around the 1780's the silhouette became smaller.

Sons Of Liberty- This is a group of merchants who united to oppose the Stamp Act of 1765. Nightly, they marched in protest in New York City, demanding liberty. These protests encouraged others to boycott British imported goods. Other people who did not belong to the group started to adopt the term "Sons of Liberty". These were tenants living on the Hudson River, which is north of New York City. These tenants refused to pay rent, and also refused to vacate the abodes they were renting. The original Sons of Liberty clarified that these actions were not honorable and these rebellions would not be tolerated by their original Sons of Liberty group. The copy-sons of liberty were soon suppressed by British troops and others. Some members of the original group included Isaac Sears, John Lamb, and Alexander McDougall.

Stays - Another term could be "boning" or "corset". This was an undergarment used by ladies which was placed over a chemise and around the torso. Usually, it encased whale-bone in fabric pockets to create a conical wrapping around the rib-cage, to cover the torso, then secured with laces. This caused the posture to be very upright.

ABOUT Wynter Sommers

Wynter Sommers is the pseudonym for an American writing team, which harnesses multiple skills in technology, research, history and education. Formally trained with a PhD in Education, Wynter Sommers blends academic classroom experience, with corporate sophistication, and a passion for developing more effective student insights through engaging storytelling.

Wynter Sommers has a heart to inspire creativity and develop critical thinking skills, all to encourage readers to make wise choices in life.

Wynter Sommers takes each story and weaves the plot with classic gripping elements, which endure throughout repeated readings, revealing new meanings each time the story is explored. The small choices a reader makes in real life could have a lasting effect in future generations. This set of stories shows the origin of not just Bjorn Esterday and Sarah Paradise, but of their ancestors and the sort of world which was established, which unfolded in each generation until Bjorn and Sarah met.

It is rewarding to learn of heartfelt, thought provoking conversations taking place globally about the characters of these books. Should the reader be presented with extraordinary circumstances, it is the sincerest wish that they act with honor, truth and integrity to overcome obstacles in real life whilst the reader hones skills of self-reliance and collaborative teamwork despite barriers outside of the reader's control. Wynter Sommers hopes you enjoy the other *Bjorn Esterday Was not Born Yesterday* stories in this series.

www.ingramcontent.com/pod-product-compliance
Lightning Source LLC
Chambersburg PA
CBHW030036030726
47500CB00001B/133